To George Goddard,
who made the world
more beautiful.

Copyright © 2002 by Michael Foreman
The rights of Michael Foreman to be identified as the author and illustrator of this work
have been asserted by him in accordance with the Copyright, Designs and Patents Act, 1988.
First published in Great Britain in 2002 by Andersen Press Ltd.,20 Vauxhall Bridge Road, London SW1V 2SA.
Published in Australia by Random House Australia Pty., 20 Alfred Street, Milsons Point, Sydney, NSW 2061.
All rights reserved. Colour separated in Switzerland by Photolitho AG, Zürich.
Printed and bound in Italy by Grafiche AZ, Verona.

10   9   8   7   6   5   4   3   2   1

British Library Cataloguing in Publication Data available.

ISBN 1 84270 219 X

This book has been printed on acid-free paper

Evie and the Man Who Helped God

Michael Foreman

Andersen Press
London

Evie loved the garden.

Especially on Mondays when George, the gardener, came.
Evie liked to help George and while they worked they
had long conversations about the garden and all the things
that grew and flew and hopped there.

George told her about the newts and frogs in the pond
and the names of all the birds who visited the garden.
Evie's favourite bird was a robin who always came
when George was there.

In Spring George held Evie up to smell the blossom and in summer he cut the grass while Evie picked flowers for the house.

In autumn Evie helped George rake up the leaves for the bonfire and plant seeds for next year.

In winter, when the pond was frozen and the frogs nowhere to be seen, the robin still came to see George. "Make sure there are always some nuts for him," said George. And the robin sat on the handle of the spade and nodded.

All winter Evie looked forward to the first signs of new things growing in her garden.

The snowdrops were always first.
Tiny drops of winter, smelling of spring.
Then came the daffodils, golden trumpets with songs of summer.

Most of all Evie looked forward to the first little splash in the pond. It told her that the first frog was awake and she knew that soon the pond would be full of leaping, diving frogs amongst the new yellow flowers of the Marsh Marigolds.

Soon tadpoles lay in shallow pools on the wide leaves of water lilies. Clouds of mayflies danced like gold dust in the warm air above the pond.

It was Evie's favourite time of year. Everything was new. Everything was growing. Everything was young.

George loved this time too. George had seen it all before. Many times. The new flowers were like old friends.

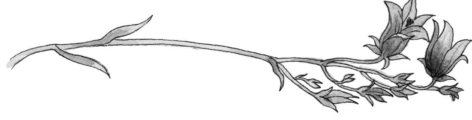

Spring was a busy time.
The grass had to be cut. George liked to
do it perfectly and he showed Evie how
to do it in long, straight lines.

She loved the smell of newly cut grass.
Some of the cut grass always blew into the
pond and Evie was careful to scoop it out
without catching any of the tadpoles.

Soon ladybirds and dragonflies
and blue butterflies, like little flakes
of sky, flittered amongst all the
colours of summer.

George said summer was a busy time
for bees but not for gardeners.

Of course, some work had to be done,
but he said it was also important
to relax in the garden.

"Just sit back and enjoy the sounds
and smells and all the colours."

And the robin sat on the spade
and nodded.

"Do you like making gardens?"
Evie asked one day. George smiled.
"I don't make gardens, Eve," he said.
"God does. I just help."
"I like helping too," said Evie.
George was the only person to call her
by her proper name.
"Eve is a good name for a gardener,"
he always said.

When Evie grew older and
started school, she only saw George
in the holidays.
"God made all things bright and
beautiful," Evie told George.
" We sang about it in school."
"So he did," said George. "And all
creatures great and small."

J136 373

But one day George did not come to the garden,
and Evie's mum said he wouldn't be coming any more.
"But who will help God on Mondays?" asked Evie.
"George will," smiled her mother. "George has gone to help
Him all the time."

Evie walked slowly around her garden. She saw lilies in pots,
waiting for George to plant out.

Evie took George's old spade from the shed. It was quite heavy but the handle was wonderfully smooth.

She planted the lilies near the pond. George always said they gave good shade for the frogs.

When she had finished,
Evie lay by the pond and watched
the frogs swimming in the shade
of the lilies.
All around her were the sounds
and the smells and all the colours
of the garden.

And the robin sat on the spade,
and nodded.